Getting it Dirty

it

Dirty

DEM SUM LEATHER

Getting It Dirty
Copyright © 2025 by Dem Sum Leather.

MILTON & HUGO L.L.C.
4407 Park Ave., Suite 5
Union City, NJ 07087, USA

Website: *www. miltonandhugo.com*
Hotline: *1- 888-778-0033*
Email: *info@miltonandhugo.com*

Ordering Information:
Quantity sales. Special discounts are granted to corporations, associations, and other organizations. For more information on these discounts, please reach out to the publisher using the contact information provided above.

Library of Congress Control Number: 2024924932
ISBN-13:   979-8-89285-367-5   [Paperback Edition]
              979-8-89285-368-2   [Digital Edition]

Rev. date: 04/07/2025

The title of the book is sure to grab your attention and where it is exactly as it sounds. This is a book for lovers who are about fun and looking to get a little more filthy in the bedroom. The art and practice of talking dirty (dirty talk) is a good way to enhancing your sexual exhibitions. Where it is not a part of your everyday personality it can be a key factor of your love making and that is an important fact. Whether a guilty pleasure or just to give it a one-time go (I would recommend more than once) it can be a boost that can help to boost or take the love making over the top.

Some of the words or phrases in this book can be substituted and many probably should depending on you or your partners comfort level. Some practice may be needed, so practice saying the phrases in your mind or out loud to yourself before you initiate them into play. But no more delay go ahead and crack this book open read, laugh and remember to Think Dirty Be Dirty!!!

Contents

Oral

This section is dedicated to oral sex. These are that you can incorporate while performing or initiating, or enjoying oral sex with your partner. Some are for encouragement and some are instructional while others are just for the sake of acknowledging the act and making you feel even more dirty.

Oral

- ❖ Suck this Dick Pussy Hoe
- ❖ Bitch Suck That Dick Real Slow And Look At Me
- ❖ Eat this Dick Bitch
- ❖ Bitch I'm trying to get ate like a steak
- ❖ Come Polish this Rifle Like You In the Army Bitch

- ❖ Come Sit on my face and use your feet to beat me off
- ❖ Suck this dick with no hands
- ❖ Spread that shit bitch let me eat that ass
- ❖ Suck my balls like a neck bone
- ❖ Suck that dick good before I poot in your face
- ❖ Gag on this dick before I fuck that asshole

- ❖ Baby you suck dick like a porn star
- ❖ Bend over so I can blow in your ass so it can blow back in my face
- ❖ Bend over I wanna smell your pussy and asshole
- ❖ Sit on my face and don't get off until you cum
- ❖ Ima tongue fuck your asshole
- ❖ I wanna make love to your ass hole with my tongue

- ❖ I could eat this pussy for breakfast
- ❖ This pussy taste like it belong to a boss bitch
- ❖ This pussy taste like it belong to a slut
- ❖ I bet this pussy taste better with a finger in your bootyhole
- ❖ You suck that dick so good your mother would be proud of you

- ❖ Say AHH

- ❖ I wanna suck your booty hole

- ❖ Girl you sucking that like its life or death

- ❖ You are so beautiful When you do that

- ❖ You are so beautiful right now

- ❖ You are most beautiful when you're doing that

- ❖ Hurry up and make me cum so I can put it in your face

- ❖ Make me cum so I can tell you I love you
- ❖ Look at me you ugly bitch
- ❖ You taste so good you need your own isle in Wal-mart
- ❖ Bend over I wanna smell your pussy and asshole

Anal

Just like allot of the speculation around the act of doing anal. These are a few ways to dirty up the experience and while some are along the rough and less than gentle side of things. Its not a one size fits all situation So customization is allowed.

Anal

- ❖ Let me Fuck you in the ass bitch
- ❖ Tell me to put it in your ass
- ❖ I like you so much I'm gonna fuck your booty hole
- ❖ Bend over so I can blow in your ass so it can blow back in my face
- ❖ Bend over I wanna smell your pussy and asshole
- ❖ Every time we do anal it feel better than the last time
- ❖ Your ass feel so good it will make the pastor sinn

Sexing
(Fucking)

Sex or sexing is done in many different ways from positions to rituals and even partners. But the act of talking dirty can help enhance the experience. And is also a way for you and your partner to be more engaging to one another To Help get the more kinky thoughts out and communicate your feelings and sensations. While letting your partner know the pleasure they are giving you. And you can let them know the pleasure you intend to give, while anticipation is a tool to have within your arsenal my suggestion is to put it to good use.

Sexing

(Fucking)

- ❖ Shut up and take this dick
- ❖ You feel this dick (if not) Call her a bitch and spit in her mouth
- ❖ Don't run from this dick, take this dick
- ❖ Who pussy this is bitch
- ❖ You better not give this good pussy to nobody

- ❖ Tell me you love this dick
- ❖ Bitch you give this good pussy away I will kill you
- ❖ Call me daddy
- ❖ O yeah mama
- ❖ Bitch shut up and take this dick
- ❖ This my Pussy Bitch
- ❖ Cum All over this dick bitch

- ❖ Let me fuck you in the ass bitch

- ❖ You like this big dick baby

- ❖ Ride this dick bitch

- ❖ Spread your ass cheeks for a bottle of liquor

- ❖ Call me sweet dick willy

- ❖ This my pussy Bitch you better never give this shit to no one

- Make me cum ima put it on your face

- Bend over so I can slap you

- Tell me to put it in your ass

- Make me cum so I can say I love you

- I love you (slap her on the ass grab throat kiss open mouth and suck her tongue)

- Look at me you ugly bitch

- ❖ Don't look at me with them dirty whore eyes you dirty whore
- ❖ You a whore (Tell me you're a whore)
- ❖ You a whore(Tell me you're a whore and you fuck for nuts)
- ❖ You a Whore(Tell me you're a whore and you love it)
- ❖ You a Whore (Tell me you're a whore who give blow jobs just to fuck)

❖ (pull out her) tell her get on her knees(put your penis in her face) tell her to smell it (then say it smell like another man's pussy) tell her put it in her mouth and clean it with her tramp ass

❖ (While fucking from behind) This pussy so good you deserve an award (pull hair hard then release) and put finger in booty hole quickly

- This pussy so good I should fuck yo ass

- You a good bitch aint you

- You a good whore I should run a train on you that's what a good bitch like

- You a good girl, I should fuck you in your ass with your good ass

- You a Nasty whore

- You a whore, I love that you a whore

- I love you cause you a whore

- ❖ You a freak cause only a freak can take this much dick
- ❖ You're a freak only a freak can keep fucking a dick this small
- ❖ You're a sexy bitch
- ❖ You're a sexy motherfucker
- ❖ You a sexy whore
- ❖ You're a slut and this some slut pussy(tell her say it to you)

❖ I love you look like a slut bitch and you are a slut bitch (tell her say she a slut bitch)

❖ I love how you look innocent but you a dirty slut and you know it

❖ You riding that dick like it's going somewhere (you're a good girl)

❖ (tell her say to you) I'm a slut and my pussy is a bottomless pit

❖ (tell her say) I live to fuck because I love to fuck

- ❖ Everytime you slap her on the ass (she should say she's a slut bitch and that's all she wanna be)
- ❖ (tell her everytime you pull her hair she say) she a bitch and need dick
- ❖ Im gonna make my dick kiss the back of your navel
- ❖ Ima fuck this pussy into a coma
- ❖ When I'm through this pussy gone ask for me by name

Texting
(Sexting)

Texting

(Females)

❖ Send your partner a picture of your underwear in a familiar but not where you are

❖ Tell him to meet you at a particular place and precise time in the back seat(make sure your clear what your intentions are)sex

- ❖ Ask how he would like to be served tonight Head, Pussy, Ass, Pussy, Head Pussy, Head, Ass

- ❖ Send him a message saying how much he turned you on this morning

- ❖ Tell him ever since you saw him all you have been thinking about is sucking his dick

- ❖ Tell him all you can think about is his dick since seeing him

- ❖ Send him a picture of something suggestive and tell him tell you the first thing that comes to his mind
- ❖ Tell him one thing that he does that you find attractive or turns you on
- ❖ Tell him one thing that is a fantasy that you want to do to him
- ❖ Send him a text that ask him how he feel about sex in the work place. Then meet him in the parking lot of his job for sex
- ❖ Send him an invitation for a date and what to bring

- ❖ Start a conversation about a sexual interest that you never shared with him
- ❖ Start a scavenger hunt with a special prize at the end
- ❖ Send him a picture everyday for a week and ask him what comes to mind for each picture and do it at the end of the day or week

Texting

(Males)

- ❖ Text her, go to the hardware store and get these things, a good screw, a good hammer and a good nail (Send her an address to where you will be and tell her this is where she can find all those things)
- ❖ Send her a Picture of your dick print in your pants and blame her
- ❖ Ask her what fruit is the most erotic to her and then tell her yours

- ❖ Tell 3 parts of her body that you find the most sexy

- ❖ Ask one place that she wants to have sex but have not / tell her one of yours and(Get it done)

- ❖ Send her pictures of 7 seven different fruits and tell her to give each fruit a day of the week /tell her a sex act that you will perform on her while she eat each fruit on each day of the week

- ❖ Send her a picture of your print and say describe in three words

- ❖ Tell her one part of her body that you have never kissed but wants to/ask how she thinks it will feel to her.

Acknowledgments

Thanks to Milton & Hugo publishing and Thanks to Anyone who always wanted to see the underdog win and A Great Deal of Appreciation To Those who were with me in Williamsburg FCI!!!